for Kate Colquhoun

...who went voling   M.W.

for Gregory   B.F.

Text copyright
© 1992 by Martin Waddell
Illustrations copyright
© 1992 by Barbara Firth

First U.S. edition 1992
First published in Great Britain
in 1992 by Walker Books Ltd., London.
ISBN 1-56402-082-7
Library of Congress Catalog Card Number 91-58755
Library of Congress Cataloging-in-Publication
information is available.

10 9 8 7 6 5 4 3 2 1

Printed and bound in Hong Kong

The illustrations in this book are
watercolor and pencil.

Candlewick Press
2067 Massachusetts Avenue
Cambridge, Massachusetts 02140

Sam Vole
and his
Brothers

Martin Waddell

illustrated by

Barbara Firth

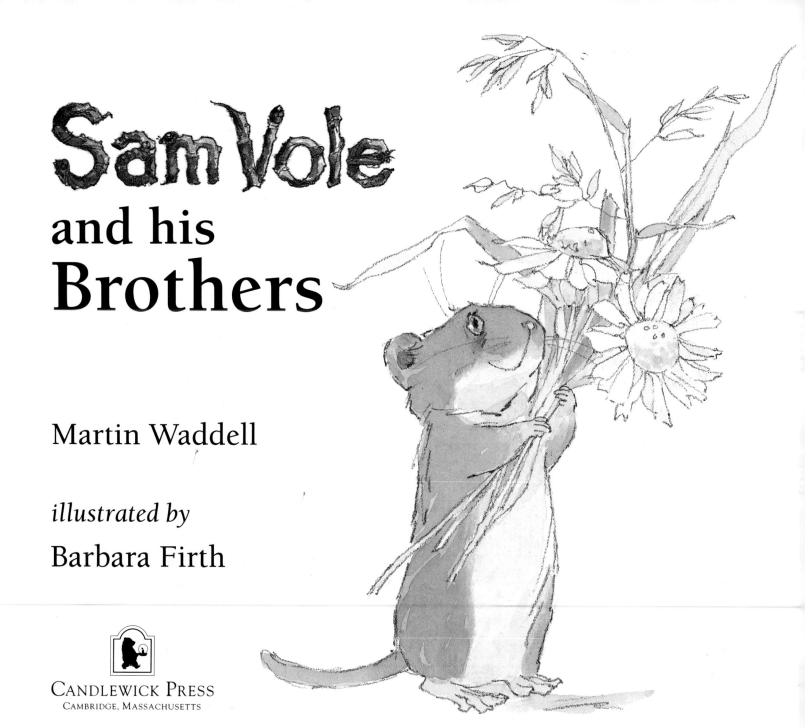

CANDLEWICK PRESS
CAMBRIDGE, MASSACHUSETTS

Sam Vole
had big brothers,
Arthur and Henry.
Sam wanted to do things
all by himself, but wherever
he went his brothers went too.

"I'm going voling for nuts,"
Sam told Mother. "I'm going
voling all by myself."

Sam went voling out in the meadow,
but Arthur and Henry went too.
They brought home more nuts than Sam,
enough for them all.
Sam gave his nuts to Mother.

"I'm going voling for grass,"
Sam told Mother.
"I'm going voling all by myself."
Sam went voling out in the meadow,
but Arthur and Henry went too.
They carried home more grass than Sam,
enough for them all.
Sam gave his grass to Mother.

"I'm going voling for daisies,"
Sam told Mother.
"I'm going voling all by myself."
Sam went voling out in the meadow,
but Arthur and Henry went too.
They picked more daisies than Sam,
enough for them all.
Sam gave his daisies to Mother.

When they all went to bed,

Sam could not sleep.

He lay awake thinking,

I want to do something all by myself.

Early the next morning he did it.
He slipped out of the house
and into the meadow,
and he went voling
alone.

He voled and he voled
all by himself
and he sang and he danced,
for he liked it so much
without brothers.

He voled and he voled
all by himself
and he ran and he jumped,
for he liked it a lot
without brothers.

He voled and he voled
all by himself
and he walked and he whistled,
for he still liked it a little
without brothers.

He voled and he voled
all by himself.
Then he stopped and he stood
and he listened.
He didn't like it at all
without brothers.

Sam sat and felt sad
without brothers.

Then he saw . . .

Arthur and Henry,
his brothers.

And Sam said,
"I've been voling alone
all by myself.
Now I'll vole with you.
You're my brothers."

And they voled around
the meadow together.

And then . . .

the brothers voled happily home.